This book belongs to:

_____

_____

Contents

First published 2006 by Brown Watson
The Old Mill, 76 Fleckney Road,
Kibworth Beauchamp, Leic LE8 0HG

ISBN: 978-0-7097-1742-3

EARLY READERS

Three Dreamtime Stories

Stories by Gill Davies

Illustrations by:
Gill Guile, Stephen Holmes,
Jane Swift and Lawrie Taylor

Brown Watson

ENGLAND

A HUNGRY DRAGON

"Oh, dear, my fire has gone out," says the Dragon. "How can I make my tea now? I am really hungry. Ooooh! I have never been so very, very hungry before."

"Dragons must be brave," he says. He gets up into a tree so no-one will see him cry.

"Brave dragons don't cry," cries Dragon. "But this one does."

Tears begin to drip off his nose. He cries so hard that he does not see the children having a picnic. Soon his big tears fall on a little girl.

"It is raining," she says, and runs off into the trees.

Then at last Dragon sees the barbecue. He jumps down.

"What luck!" says Dragon.

In no time at all Dragon has lit
his fire again. He looks so happy
that the children come out
from the trees.

"Please eat with us," they say.
"We have never had a picnic
with a dragon before."

They all eat well. Soon
Dragon is full. He hops off
home again, as happy as
can be.

KEY WORDS

be	how
before	never
been	nose
begin	off
dear	on
eat	really
full	soon
hops	well

WHAT CAN YOU SEE HERE?

Dragon

trees

notice

barbecue

girl

THE SAD CLOWN

Clown is sad. "Look, Clown is crying," says Becky Bear.

"He has been crying all day," says Ben Bear.

"Poor old Clown," says Father. "You left him in the garden. You left him on the grass. You left him in the rain. Now he is wet and tired . . . but let me see what I can do."

The next day, the two little bears run to Father's workshop to see if Clown is better.

They hear Father Bear say, "This old thing is no good. I shall put it in the bin."

"No! Stop! Don't!" says Ben, running in.

"No! Stop! Don't!" says Becky. "Don't put Clown in the bin."

"I am talking about this old clock," says Father . . . "Not Clown. Clown is as good as new now. See."

Clown is dry. Clown is clean. Clown is happy. Ben and Becky are happy too.

"Thanks," they say. "Thank you, thank you, thank you!"

Then they hug happy Clown and take him home.

KEY WORDS

all	run
can	sad
day	say
he	stop
look	then
no	they
not	this
put	too

WHAT CAN YOU SEE HERE?

Clown

Becky Bear

Father Bear

Mother Bear

Clock

SCARY SCARECROW

Donkey and Sam Scarecrow are the best of friends. They always stay side by side and play together. One day they hear the sheep go, "Baa! Baa! Help! Baa! Help!"

"What is going on?" asks Donkey.

"Look," says Sam. "Some very bad men are trying to take our sheep away. We must try to stop them."

23

Donkey trots across the field. Sam Scarecrow hops across the field. They get into the back of the shed. The bad men do not see them.

Then Donkey brays and stamps. He snorts and kicks. Dust flies up everywhere. Sam jumps. He waves and shouts. His big coat flaps up and down. More dust flies up.

The bad men do not know who or what it is.

"Help! Run. We must get away," they cry. "Something scary is after us." They run out of the shed. They jump into a car. Soon they are far, far away.

"Thank you," baa the sheep. "Now we are safe again. You two are very clever – and very funny too."

KEY WORDS

always	into
and	jumps
bad	must
funny	our
get	says
go	take
going	them
help	what

WHAT CAN YOU SEE HERE?

sheep

shed

scarecrow

bucket

wood